STAY, FANG

STAY, FANG

by Barbara Shook Hazen
illustrated by Leslie Holt Morrill

ATHENEUM   1990   NEW YORK

I have a dog. His name is Fang.
He likes balls and bones and, best of all,

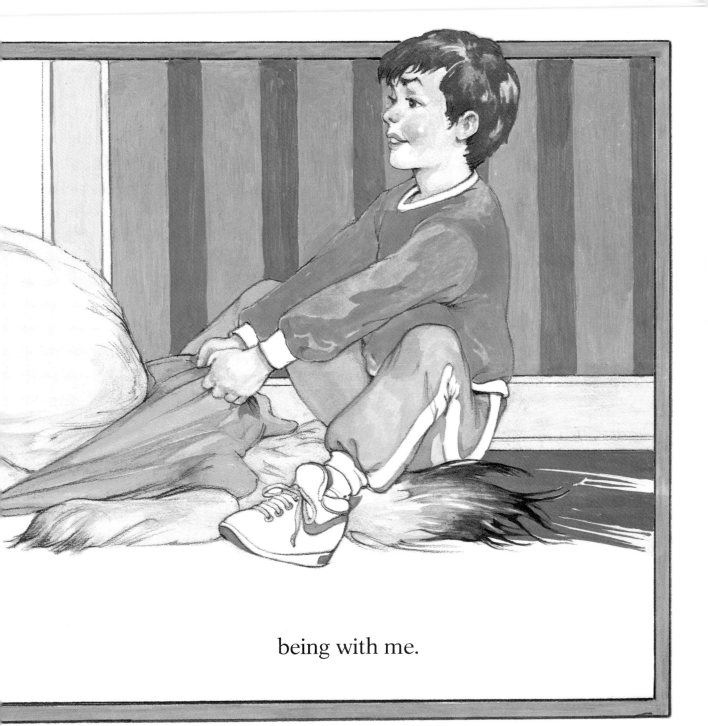

being with me.

What Fang doesn't like is staying.
He doesn't like it when I go someplace
he doesn't get to go— like school,

or my cousin Eddie's overnight.

He doesn't like it when I take him someplace
where I get to go in, but he has to stay outside—
like the mini-mart, or the library,

or the park playground,
where my friend Bernie and I go a lot.

I always hug Fang and say, "Stay,"
before I loop his leash around the fence.
Fang always gives me his sad look.
So I always pat him and tell him, "I understand,"
because I do, even if it is different with a dog.

Then he whines and whimpers,
and paws the ground and pulls at his leash,
and acts like I'm never coming back,

until I come back and untangle his leash.
Then he wags his tail and wriggles and licks me
like I've been gone forever.

So I hug Fang again and tell him again,
"I'll only be a little while.
I love you and I always come back.
But you have got to learn to stay."

Fang looks at me like he understands.
But he doesn't. The second I leave,
he starts whining and whimpering
and pawing and pulling all over again—
sometimes a lot of agains, until we have to go home.

Fang's even worse on school days.
I always hug him before I go.
On the way out, I wave and say,
"See you later."

But Fang doesn't act like there will be a later.
Mom says that after I'm gone,
Fang sits by the window and watches and
waits for me to come back.

Once he howled so loudly a neighbor complained.

Once he got mad at me for going,
and went in my room, and chewed my sneaker,
and knocked down my moon city.

And once he jumped out of the window
and followed me to school,
which meant I had to go back,

which made me late.

I've tried everything.
I've tried sneaking out of the house
and not saying, "Stay," or telling Fang
where I'm going.
But that doesn't work, because Fang's too smart.

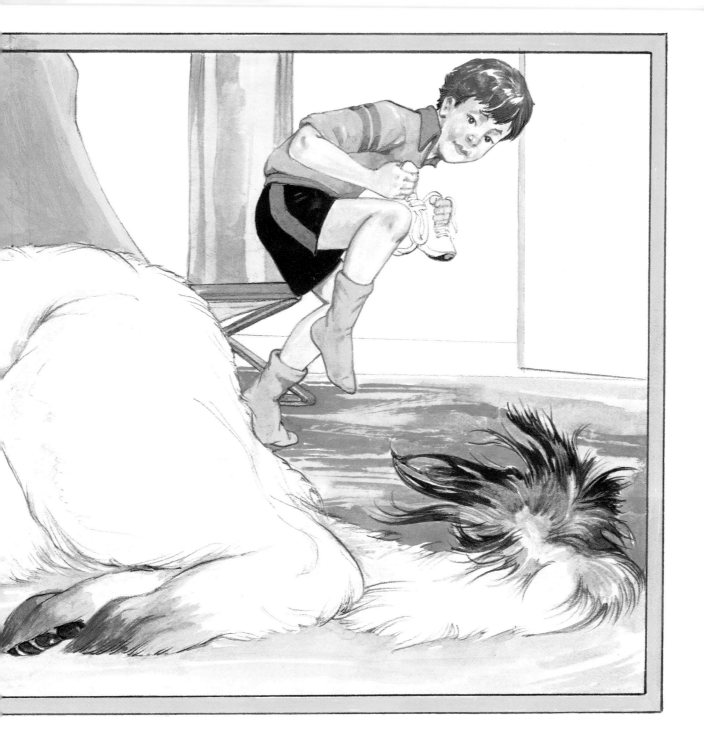

I've tried leaving the TV on
and giving Fang squeak toys
so he'll have something to play with while I'm gone.

That doesn't work either, because
Fang wants to play with me.

I've tried explaining, "Look, Fang,
there are just some places dogs can't go,
the way there are some places kids can't go.
But wherever I go, whatever I do,
I'll be back. Always and no matter what—
even if the game has extra innings,

or I stop by at Bernie's
or walk home the longer way. Okay?"

Only it isn't okay. Nothing works.
Fang still hates to stay.
And I still keep on trying.
I keep on saying, "Stay, Fang,"
and hugging him and telling him,
"I love you and I'll always be back."

Then one day, when I get home,
Mom greets me. "Guess what?" she says.
"Fang whimpered once, and then he settled down.
He played with his toy and took a nap. And so did I."

I am so happy I ruffle Fang's fur and hug
him hard and say, "See, I knew you could do it.

Staying's not so bad.

It can even be fun."

Atheneum
Macmillan Publishing Company
866 Third Avenue, New York, NY 10022
Collier Macmillan Canada, Inc.
First Edition
Printed in the United States of America
10 9 8 7 6 5 4 3 2 1

Library of Congress Cataloging-in-Publication Data
Hazen, Barbara Shook.
    Stay, Fang / by Barbara Shook Hazen; illustrated by Leslie Holt
Morrill. —1st ed. p. cm.
    Summary: A dog who likes to follow his master everywhere finally
learns to "stay."
    ISBN 0–689–31599–6
    [1. Dogs—Fiction.] I. Morrill, Leslie H., ill. II. Title.
PZ7.H314975Ss 1990 [E]—dc20
89-32359 CIP AC